To Peter, my favourite fisherman
S.J—P.

Photoset by Deltatype Ltd, Ellesmere Port
Printed in Italy
for J.M. Dent & Sons Ltd
91 Clapham High Street
London SW4 7TA

British Library Cataloguing in Publication Data
Bradman, Tony, 1954 –
That's not a fish.
I. Title II. Jenkin – Pearce, Susie
823'.914

*The illustrations for this book were prepared using
ink line and water-colour*

That's not a Fish!

TONY BRADMAN

Illustrated by

**SUSIE
JENKIN-PEARCE**

Dent Children's Books

London

This is the story of Jack,
a little boy whose Dad liked fishing.

One Sunday, Dad took Jack
to Granny's.
She was going to look after
him while Dad went fishing.

"I wish *I* could fish," Jack said.
"OK, Jack," said Dad.
"I'll take you . . . next week."

The idea made Jack's eyes pop
and his skin tingle.
He was so pleased he couldn't
even *speak*.

Jack could hardly wait for next Sunday.
He thought he'd better start getting ready straight away.

On Monday, quick as a flash, Jack made a fishing rod,
with a stick and a piece of string. Dad gave him a hook.

"*Now* I can fish," Jack said.

But where can a little fisherman fish? On Tuesday, Jack splashed and fished in the kitchen sink . . . and caught something!

"That's not a fish!" Jack said.

On Wednesday, Jack played in the garden.
He sploshed and fished in a bucket, and
found a *very* strange creature.

"That's not a fish!" Jack said.

On Thursday, Dad took Jack to the shops.
They bought some new Wellington
boots and an anorak to keep him dry.

On the way home Jack splished
and fished in a great big puddle, and
something took his hook.

"That's not a fish!" Jack said.

On Friday, Jack said . . .
"Yippee! The weekend's here!"

He splashed and sploshed and
splished and fished in the bath.
He made a mess, but he caught
something in the end.

"That's not a fish!" Jack said.

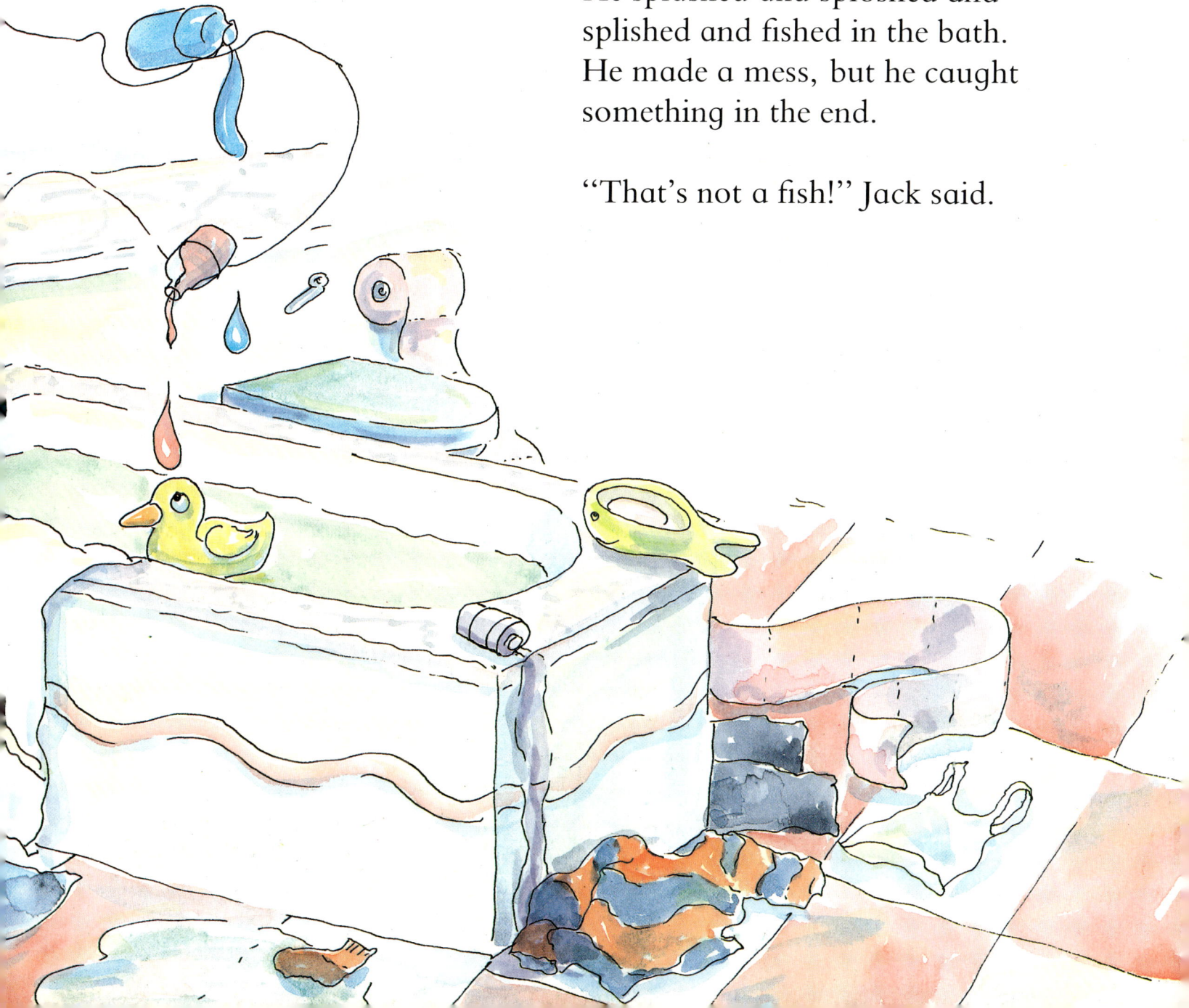

Saturday was Jack's last chance
to get plenty of practice, so he
did lots and lots of fishing.
He fished in his cupboard . . .

he fished in his drawers . . .

he fished in his toy basket . . .

he fished in his bed.

"That's not a fish!" Jack said.
"That's Ted!"

That night, Jack dreamed of fishing,
Jack dreamed of fish, Jack dreamed
of rods and lines and still Jack
wished . . .

"But that's not a fish!" Jack said.

Jack woke up on Sunday morning. The big day had arrived!
They got up so early it was still dark. Dad made a picnic,
and Jack helped him load all their stuff in the car.

Jack kept his rod with him . . .
and fished the hat right off
Dad's head!
"That's not a fish!" Jack said.

They came to a river, where lots
of men sat.

Jack and his Dad found a spot.
They set up their rods, then the
rain poured down. It splashed and
splished in the river. It sploshed on
the ground.

But Jack and his Dad didn't care.
They were happy just being
together, and they fished, and
fished, and fished . . .

"That's not a fish!" Jack said.

At last it was time to go home. They stopped at Granny's
to get warm and dry. Dad chatted to Granny.

But Jack went off to do some fishing.

He fished in Granny's bag,
and at last he found something
that made his eyes pop
and his skin tingle . . .

"That's . . . A FISH!" Jack said.

And Granny cooked the fish for tea.